DAVID J. PLANT
HUNGRY ROSCOE

Flying Eye Books

London - New York

"I'm *starving!*" said Roscoe.

"I've had enough of eating rotten junk,"
he told his friend Benjy. They both lived in
a park in the middle of a big city.

"What I wouldn't give for a *lovely* bit
of fish or some *fresh, juicy* fruit."

"I don't know what you're fussing about,"
said Benjy. "There's plenty here to go round."
"Bleargh!" groaned Roscoe.

"Why don't you try the zoo?" suggested Benjy.
"I've heard the animals there get fresh food every day."
"Good idea!" said Roscoe.

So Roscoe entered the zoo...

...all of a sudden, he came upon a bucket
brimming with enough food to last him all week.

But Roscoe hadn't considered that
the food was meant for someone else.

"That's not for pests like you!" growled the zookeeper.
He was not a good-tempered man.

Bop! Roscoe got the boot.

"It didn't go too well, I assume?" asked Benjy. "Maybe the zoo wasn't such a good idea after all."

"It was an *excellent* idea! It's just that the food in there is meant for the zoo animals," replied Roscoe.

"So *I* need to look like one!"

And so, using:
an umbrella...

...four tin cans...

...and some
orange peel...

...Roscoe created his disguise.
He was no longer Roscoe the raccoon, he was now...

Roscoe the tortoise!

Just as feeding time was approaching,
Roscoe wobbled into the tortoise enclosure
and tried his best to blend in.

Sadly, he didn't fool the zookeeper.
"Back to cause trouble again, are we?" he snarled.

Biff! For the second time that day, Roscoe got the boot.
"*Last warning!* Show up again and you'll be sorry!"

"Maybe you should take a hint," said Benjy.

"No..." Roscoe muttered.
"I just need a better disguise."

This time, he collected:
an ice-cream cone...

...and a dirty,
old jacket...

...and became...

Roscoe the penguin!

Again, just as feeding time was approaching,
Roscoe made his entrance at the penguin pool.
"Squawk!" he announced.

But, *yet again*, the zookeeper saw through Roscoe's disguise. "No more warnings! You're going to get it now!" he yelled.

Roscoe ran this way and that way.
The zookeeper was hot on his heels!

Finally, he managed to slip out of sight.
"Phew!" sighed Roscoe. "That was close!"

"Pssssssssstt!"

someone
whispered from nearby...

It was the monkeys. "Hey! We noticed you've been looking for a snack. The zookeeper left a *load* of food in here – more than *we* can eat. If you can get the key to our cage, it's *yours*."

"This is my chance!" thought Roscoe.

Using his best sneaking skills, he crept towards the zookeeper...

...and snatched his keys.

"Nice work!"

"Nice work!"   "Good job!"   "Well done!"

chattered the monkeys, as Roscoe
unlocked the door with a *ker-click!*

"Thanks, guys! How can I ever repay you?" drooled Roscoe.
"Don't worry about it," chuckled the monkeys.

What Roscoe didn't realize was that monkeys...

...love nothing more than causing mischief.

Using the stolen keys, the monkeys unlocked the doors...

...of *every* animal in the *entire* zoo.

What followed was not pretty.

The zookeeper had to spend the rest of the day rounding up the escaped animals.

Not all of them returned willingly.

By the evening he was exhausted and had long since missed his dinner.

Roscoe thought he looked hungry.

"Maybe I'll pop back tomorrow," Roscoe called to the zookeeper.

"If it's not too much trouble!"

Burp!